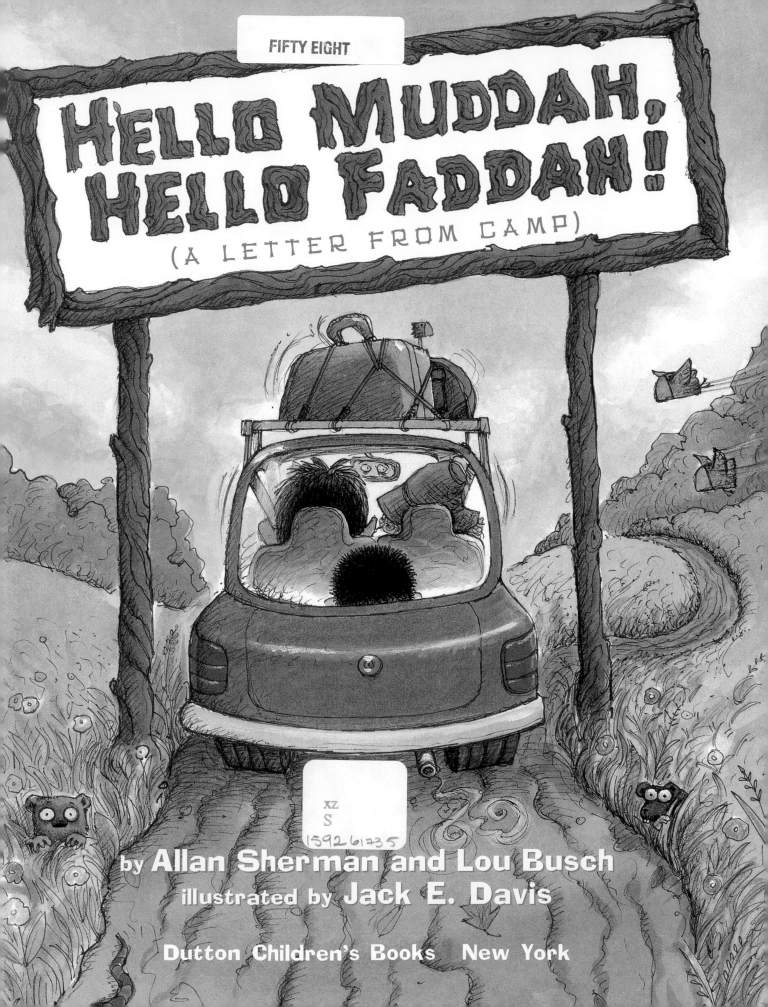

HELLO MUDDAH, HELLO FADDAH!
(A LETTER FROM CAMP)

by **Allan Sherman** and **Lou Busch**
illustrated by **Jack E. Davis**

Dutton Children's Books   New York

For Lucy, Janey, and Vincent
J.E.D.

Words by Allan Sherman
Music by Lou Busch
© 1963 (Renewed 1991) WB Music Corp. and Burning Bush Music.
Lyrics reprinted by permission of Warner Bros. Publications.

Illustrations copyright © 2004 by Jack E. Davis

CIP Data is available.

Published in the United States 2004 by Dutton Children's Books,
a division of Penguin Young Readers Group
345 Hudson Street, New York, New York 10014
www.penguin.com
Designed by Richard Amari

Manufactured in China
First Edition
3 5 7 9 10 8 6 4 2
ISBN 0-525-46942-7

Hello Muddah, hello Faddah!
Here I am at Camp Granada.

Camp is very entertaining,

and they say we'll have some
fun if it stops raining.

I went hiking with Joe Spivy.

WATCH FOR QUICKSAND

CAMP GRANADA

He developed poison ivy.

You remember Leonard Skinner?

All the counselors
hate the waiters,

and the head coach
wants no sissies,
so he reads to us from
something called *Ulysses*.

Now I don't want
this to scare ya,
but my bunkmate
has malaria.

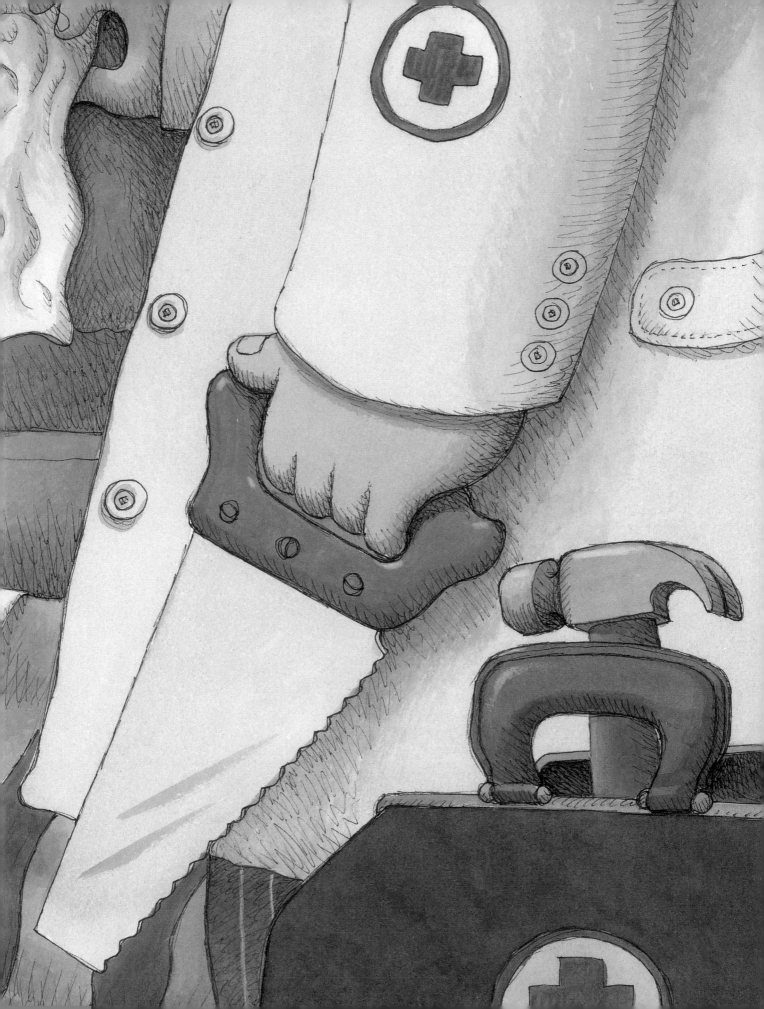

You remember Jeffrey Hardy?
They're about to organize a
searching party.

Take me home, oh Muddah, Faddah, take me home. I hate Granada.

Don't leave me out in the forest where I might get eaten by a bear.

Take me home, I promise
I will not make noise
or mess the house with other boys.

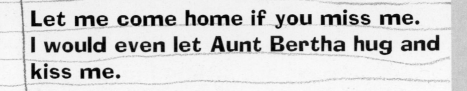

Let me come home if you miss me.
I would even let Aunt Bertha hug and
kiss me.

Playing baseball,
gee that's better.

Muddah, Faddah, kindly disregard this letter.